A MURDER FOR MAX

A MAXINE BENSON MYSTERY

John Lawrence Reynolds

RAVEN BOOKS
an imprint of
ORCA BOOK PUBLISHERS

Library and Archives Canada Cataloguing in Publication

Reynolds, John Lawrence, author
A murder for Max / John Lawrence Reynolds.
(Rapid reads)

Issued also in print and electronic formats.
ISBN 978-1-4598-1059-4 (pbk.).—ISBN 978-1-4598-1061-7 (pdf).—
ISBN 978-1-4598-1060-0 (epub)

I. Title. II. Series: Rapid reads
PS8585.E94M87 2016   C813'.54   C2016-900528-3
C2016-900529-1

First published in the United States, 2016
Library of Congress Control Number: 2016931822

Summary: Maxine Benson, police chief in a small town, sets out to solve
the murder of a local bad boy in this work of crime fiction. (RL 3.6)

MIX
Paper from
responsible sources
FSC® C103214

*Orca Book Publishers is dedicated to preserving the environment and has
printed this book on Forest Stewardship Council® certified paper.*

Orca Book Publishers gratefully acknowledges the support for
its publishing programs provided by the following agencies:
the Government of Canada through the Canada Book Fund and the
Canada Council for the Arts, and the Province of British Columbia
through the BC Arts Council and the Book Publishing Tax Credit.

Cover design by Jenn Playford
Cover photography by iStock.com

ORCA BOOK PUBLISHERS
www.orcabook.com

Printed and bound in Canada.

19 18 17 16 • 4 3 2 1

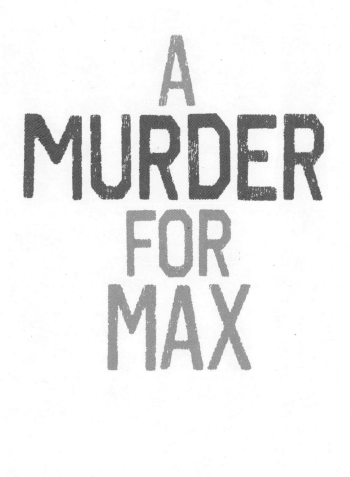

A MURDER FOR MAX

For Pat and Phil Scott

ONE

Police Chief Maxine Benson had to prove something to the people of Port Ainslie. They did not doubt that she could perform most of her duties. And until now they had not questioned the wisdom of hiring a woman as police chief. But Maxine feared this all might end when Billy Ray Edwards was found shot to death in his garage.

"Sure," she could hear them say, "you do fine with break-ins and drivers who speed through town. And you lock up Bop Chadwick when he drinks too much rum on Saturday night. And you handled that

1

three-car smashup last New Year's Eve. But this is *murder!*"

"Bop" Chadwick had been christened Bruce Olivier Pratt, which was a mouthful. As a young man, he hated all three given names. So when signing his name he used his initials only, and B. O. P. Chadwick became "Bop." Bop married a Toronto girl and moved there. Ten years later he returned to Port Ainslie, homeless and jobless and with a thirst for rum, and the nickname seemed to fit. Everyone liked Bop. And everyone blamed the Big City Woman for Bop's troubles. But no one knew for sure. And Bop wasn't talking.

Some people would expect Max to report Billy Ray's murder to the Ontario Provincial Police. That's what other towns in Muskoka District did with major crimes. But if she asked the OPP to solve Billy Ray's murder, she feared they would take over the whole case and send her home to have a nice cup of tea. She would feel like a child being told she couldn't play with the big kids.

Would this really happen? Maybe, maybe not. But Maxine Benson had seen how male cops could act around women. Even women who wore a police badge like hers. Her badge might say *Chief*, but she believed this wouldn't keep them from looking down on her.

She refused to put up with that. She had spent too much time proving she could do all the things expected of a police chief. And she did not want anyone to think she couldn't deal with a murder herself. Especially the murder of a thug like Billy Ray Edwards. So she intended to solve it on her own. Or at least try.

———

Almost two years had passed since Maxine Benson was named police chief in Port

Ainslie. It had been two years of hard work to show the town councilors they had not made a mistake when they gave her the job.

There had been doubts at the start. A lot of doubts. Many were based on the fact that she was a woman. For some people in town, that was reason enough to wonder if she was up to the job.

Most of the town councilors liked Maxine as soon as they met her. Many were ready to sign her up right away. In a letter to the council, the chief of the Toronto police force praised Max, saying she would make a first-rate chief. The council was impressed.

There was only one problem. The council had been ready to hire a gruff, gray-haired man with a deep voice and a cold stare. Instead, they were about to give the job to a slim woman who spoke softly and smiled sweetly. Everyone who met Max said she was "nice" and "polite" and even "pretty." The fact was, she looked more like grade-school teacher than a police chief.

So why did they hire her?

The fact that four of seven councilors were women had much to do with it. They did not believe it took a deep voice and gray hair to keep the peace. They thought other things counted as well. Things like being nice to people and using soft talk instead of loud threats.

And so she became Port Ainslie Chief of Police Maxine Benson, "Chief Max" to everyone in town. This bothered her at first. She hated being called Max. All her life she had wanted a "normal" woman's name, like Susan or Emma or Hannah. As a teenager, she had told her mother over and over how much she hated her name.

Your name, her mother had replied, *is lovely and elegant. It comes from* Maximus, *meaning "great." So there you are. You are great.*

To the kids at school, Maxine said, *I am Max, which is not lovely and elegant. It is short and ugly, and it sounds like a tattooed guy who drives a truck.*

She could have changed her name as an adult, but she was afraid it might insult her parents. She loved them very much, even if they had given her a name she hated. So she remained Max. She didn't like it, but she grew used to it.

None of this mattered much now that Port Ainslie had a murder on its hands. Would the people in town doubt that Max could solve it? She was afraid they would. She needed to prove she could deal with serious crimes. Even a murder. And she intended to. But there was a problem.

When Max was hired, the town council had told her the OPP was to deal with any and all major crimes. *Major crimes* meant anything more serious than theft and speeding. Based on the small size of the

Port Ainslie Police Force, this made sense. In fact, calling it a *force* was a stretch. Max was expected to keep the peace in and around Port Ainslie with a staff of just two. One was Constable Henry Wojak. The other was the office manager, sixty-eight-year-old Margie Burns.

Henry Wojak had grown up in Port Ainslie and joined the police after high school. He had roots in the town and had never wanted to go anywhere else. The farthest he had ever traveled in his life was to Montreal for a weekend. There he learned four French words. One of them, he learned later, was obscene.

Margie Burns brought her knitting to work with her. Sometimes she brought homemade cupcakes as well. Margie's job was to answer the phone, keep the books and lock prisoners in the two jail cells. Anyone who wondered if a sixty-eight-year-old grandmother could perform such duties had not met Margie. As a young woman, she had won contests in martial arts and could still place an armlock on a man who did not want to be put behind bars. In less time than it took him to say *I'm not going!* he would find himself in a jail cell. Margie would smile as she walked away. Sometimes she'd jingle the keys of the cell door for him to hear. Word of Margie, it was said, had spread far and wide beyond the town. *Do not mess with the old woman in Port Ainslie*, a lot of rough men were warned. *She could break your arm and laugh about it.*

Max could have had two constables to assist her instead of just Henry Wojak. She chose a new police cruiser instead.

The town had two cruisers when it hired Max. She told town council the two were really just one and a half cars. The newest was two years old and in good shape. The other was over ten years old, and been driven more than three hundred thousand miles. Its paint had faded, and the driver's door did not quite close. The muffler was tied in place with a coat hanger. "And the siren doesn't work," Max said when she asked town council to buy a new police car. The horn was one of the few things on the car that worked.

That should be enough for cruising around town, a male councilor said.

No, it is not, Max said. *Everyone gets out of the way when they hear a siren. No one moves when you honk your horn*. Max said if the town did not buy a new police car, she would not take the job.

The council said it could not afford to buy a new police car. Max said that without a new cruiser, she couldn't do all the things expected of her.

It looked like the town would have a rusty police car that was nearly always silent in an emergency. And it would not have Max as police chief. One member of town council had an idea. He said there was money in the budget to hire a second constable to help the new police chief. *If we don't hire one*, he said, *we can buy you a brand-new cruiser with all the bells, whistles and sirens you want.*

So Max had two choices. She could run a police force with two constables, Margie and one and a half police cars. Or she could do the job with just Henry and Margie and two police cars, one of them brand new. She could even have *POLICE CHIEF* painted on the new cruiser's door.

You have one other choice, another male council member said to Max. *You can find some other town that will hire a woman as police chief.*

The female members of council told him he had no respect for women.

I'm just being honest, he said. *She doesn't need another constable or a new car. She can do her job with one guy and Margie Burns. Margie is worth two people on her own. Most of the crime in this town is all about making noise and stealing bicycles. Sometimes old Bop Chadwick drinks rum in the park. That's it.* He pointed at Max. *The two of you and Margie should be able to handle that.*

You need to be ready for more serious crimes, Max said. *This is a peaceful town, but you have to expect bad things to happen now and then.*

Bad things? the councilor said. *Like what? A mugging? A murder?*

Yes, Max said. *That's just what I mean.*

The councilor laughed at the idea that a murder could occur in Port Ainslie. *I don't expect anything like that to happen in this pretty little town of ours,* he said. *But if it does, you agree to let the Ontario Provincial Police take over. How's that?*

Max knew that calling on the OPP for help in cases like murder made sense. But she still did not like the councilor's words.

She only agreed because she wanted the job badly. Maybe too badly.

A mile or two of lakeshore spread on either side of Port Ainslie, so the area to be covered by the police was larger than it appeared. All in all, it covered almost four miles along the north shore of Granite Lake, and two miles north. It included the south face of Granite Mountain, the highest hill in Muskoka. Calling it a mountain was like calling a chicken an ostrich. The town's slogan, "Home of Muskoka Magic," was another stretch of the truth. The only magic in town happened when Henry Wojak did card tricks for Margie on a slow day at the police station. But it was a pretty place. Everyone agreed on that.

Max had first come to Port Ainslie for a holiday with her parents when she was ten years old. The town had seemed like heaven to the young city girl. At age forty-three, with a broken marriage to get over, she saw the chance to live and work there too good to resist.

She had left Toronto to escape heartbreak and stress. She wanted out of the politics of big-city police work. The cottage she found at Willow Cove, on the lakeshore west of Port Ainslie, was perfect. She loved the idea of drifting to sleep to the cries of loons, and waking to watch the sun rise over Granite Lake.

Max had spent fifteen years as a police officer in Toronto. Those years had taken their toll. For eight of them, she had been married to a man who was a good golfer, an okay cop and a poor husband. Now she wanted to forget her life in Toronto. She would work with Henry Wojak and Margie Burns. She would have a shiny police cruiser to patrol the town and the area around it. And she would go home to Willow Cove each night.

Don't forget, a councilor warned when she took the job as police chief. *Call the* OPP *in Cranston when you need help. They can be here in half an hour. If the bridge isn't stuck.*

He meant the lift bridge over Cold River, raised to let boats pass under the highway. About twice a week, the bridge got stuck in the raised position. When this happened, it stayed there until the gears could be fixed. That could take hours. Meanwhile, highway access between Cranston and Port Ainslie was cut off. Half of the people in the area wanted a new bridge, no matter how much it cost. The other half said the bridge was part of history and should not be replaced. Neither side would budge, so nothing was done.

———

For almost two years, Max, Margie and Henry had kept the peace in Port Ainslie. Which wasn't hard. Max had evenings to relax at her cottage on the lake. Henry found time to show card tricks to tourists he met on Main Street. Margie knitted jackets for every new baby in town. And no one found a reason to complain about the town's police force. Not once did Max think of calling on the OPP.

Everyone in town was pleased with her work as the only woman police chief in Muskoka. Many even bragged about it. There was no glass ceiling in Port Ainslie, they boasted.

But, of course, Max had never had to solve a murder on her own.

Until now.

TWO

No one believed a murder could happen in pretty Port Ainslie. But when it did, no one was surprised that Billy Ray Edwards was the victim.

The truth was, almost nobody liked Billy Ray. Lots of people in town hated him. Someone hated him enough to shoot him in his own garage.

As a young man, Billy Ray had not been hated. People in Port Ainslie were too nice to hate someone just for who they were. Until his teenage years, Billy Ray had been just another kid who loved fishing and baseball and hated school. But somewhere around age sixteen he became a hoodlum, and he seemed to stay that way. When Billy Ray was twenty years old, his parents died in a car accident. Their son did not act as though he missed them. Instead, he became even more wild than before.

For a while the townsfolk put up with him. Many felt sorry he had been made an orphan by the accident. Besides, they said, every town had someone who didn't fit in. Even when Billy Ray bought a noisy motorcycle and rode it through town late at night, some people said it wasn't so bad. Billy Ray grew a beard and wore shirts with dirty words on them. The same people said it was just the way things were these days. Boys said and did things these days they would not have said and done years ago. Maybe he will grow up and change, they said.

But the only way Billy Ray changed was to become worse.

Billy Ray's parents had saved a lot of money over the years, and their son got all of it when they died. He also got the family home, which was the nicest property in town. On the shore of the lake, it included a sandy beach and many shade trees.

Billy Ray didn't care about sand or lawns or trees. He wanted to ride noisy motorcycles and have noisy parties with noisy friends. And he did. For a while. Then he married a woman named Deborah, and everyone hoped he would settle down. But it didn't last. When Deborah left him, he became even angrier and harder to get along with.

None of this mattered until a large firm said they planned to build a new resort in town. That's when people said they had had as much of Billy Ray Edwards as they could take.

The company said the resort would be the most attractive in all of Muskoka.

Maybe in all of Canada. It would cost a hundred million dollars, and be open twelve months of the year.

The resort would change Port Ainslie for the better. People would visit the town in spring for the flower festival, and in summer for swimming and boating. In autumn they would come to see the fall colors. Winter would bring them to ski down Granite Mountain. The restaurant alone would attract people to the area twelve months of the year. At least fifty people would work at the resort full-time, most from Port Ainslie and all earning good salaries.

Everyone agreed the resort would make the town more attractive. Better than that, it would make it wealthy. Ivan Curic, who ran the biggest real-estate office in town, said the resort could make Port Ainslie the richest place in all of Muskoka.

People knew how important the new resort would be to them. They all agreed to support the idea.

All but Billy Ray Edwards.

Billy Ray still lived in the house he grew up in, on the shore of the lake. The house had a perfect view of the lake and the best beach in the area. That's why it was where the Toronto company planned to build the resort. All of Billy Ray's neighbors agreed to sell their land. By June the resort company was ready to start building. All they needed was Billy Ray to agree to a price and sell his land.

Billy Ray would not agree to anything.

It wasn't the money. The company offered Billy Ray more than they had offered to anyone else. When Billy Ray said no, they raised their offer over and over, all the way to one million dollars.

Billy Ray still said no.

Someone from the company told Billy Ray he could have a job at the new resort every summer. He could be a lifeguard, or mow the lawn, or be a security guard. Whatever he did, he would draw a good salary. And still have a million dollars in the bank.

Billy Ray told him to get lost.

The company's lawyer said he would look for a legal way to force Billy Ray to sell.

Billy Ray said he would shoot anybody who came onto his land.

This brought Max and Henry to visit Billy Ray and warn him about making threats. *I am just taking care of what is mine*, Billy Ray told them.

You are being a fool, Max said to him. *Until now you have been a law-abiding fool. But if you make more threats like that one, you will find yourself in a jail cell. So try to stay out of trouble.*

I'll stay where I want to be, Billy Ray said with a sneer. *Which is right here. No broad with a badge is going to tell me what to do. Police chief or not.*

Max had dealt with tough guys before. She ignored his threat and said she did not want to come back to talk to him again.

Come back anytime, Billy Ray said with a cold smile. *Next time bring some wine. And leave that loser at the station.* He meant Henry Wojak.

Somebody is going to shut his big mouth for good, Henry said as he and Max drove away from Billy Ray's house.

I'm going to pretend I didn't hear that, Max said.

But after Billy Ray was found dead, she couldn't help remembering it.

———

I can't figure Billy Ray out, Max said to Margie after telling her of Billy Ray's threat. *What makes him act like that?*

It comes natural, Margie said. *Some people are natural athletes. Billy Ray is a natural pain in the neck. He didn't start out that way. When he was young, maybe five years old, he was a sweet little boy. Now he is just an awful person who nobody wants around.*

Brenda Karp said this wasn't true all the time. *Billy Ray can be nice when he wants to be,* she told Max one day. Brenda would know. About a year before word of the new resort was heard, Billy Ray's wife walked out on him. Brenda moved in a month later. *I guess I always liked bad boys*, she had said when people asked her why. Billy Ray fit the image of a bad boy. He had plenty of muscles, rode a loud motorcycle and liked to scare people. *If he tries hard*, Brenda said, *he can be sweet*. Then she added, *Trouble is, he won't try hard enough.*

From the day she moved in, Brenda started to repair Billy Ray's house. The rooms had not seen a drop of fresh paint in years. *I gave the place a woman's touch*, Brenda said. *It looked so much better when I was done.*

But when the work was finished, Billy Ray told Brenda he didn't want her around. He told her to take her things and get out. When she said she wanted to be paid for the work she had done, Billy Ray became violent. That's when Brenda called Margie to say she was scared for her life. Max and Henry came to talk to Billy Ray. They told Brenda it would be best if she left, and she rushed off to pack her clothes.

Max turned to Billy Ray. *If you make one threat to Brenda*, she said, *I will put you in jail.*

You and who else? he said.

Me and Margie, Max said. Billy Ray made no reply. He knew about Margie.

Max had some advice for Brenda as she was leaving. *The best thing you can do now*, she said, *is find yourself a better man.* Then she said, *Which should not be hard to do.*

It wasn't. A few weeks later Brenda moved in with Seth Torsney, who ran a garden nursery in town. But she and Billy Ray were not finished yet. In her rush to leave, Brenda had left some jewelry at his house, a few rings and bracelets. She asked for them back, but he laughed at her. When she tried to sue him, a lawyer said it was not a good idea. It was cheap jewelry, after all, and not worth the effort.

It was worth the effort to Brenda. Some of the rings were her late mother's. Seth called Billy Ray to demand Brenda's jewelry. Billy Ray told Seth that if he set foot on his property, he would come face to face with a loaded shotgun.

When Seth went to Max about the threat, Max and Henry paid another visit to Billy Ray. *That ain't a threat*, Billy Ray said. *It's a promise.* Billy Ray was a tall man with a full beard and a voice deep enough to have its own echo. *Don't care if you put me in jail*, Billy Ray said. *Nobody's tellin' me what to do. Ever. About anything.*

Max let him off with another warning.

Everyone knew Billy Ray could be a jerk. But not everyone knew why he would not sell his home for the million dollars offered by the resort firm. This was more than the price he might get on the open market. Why not take it and call himself a millionaire? Then, some folks hoped, he would move away to the big city. Anywhere but here.

Part of the reason was his stubborn streak. But there was more to it than that. Before she married Billy Ray, his wife, Deborah, had him sign a deal that would give half of all he owned to her should the marriage end. She thought it would make him a better husband. It did not. But that didn't matter now. If he sold his land before the divorce came through, Deborah would get half of all the cash. If the land was sold after the divorce, her share would be much less. So she was in no hurry to start the divorce. As soon as Billy Ray sold the land, she would ask for half of the money for the land. And she would get it.

But the company that was to build the new resort lost its patience. On Monday the company said it would take its money and go somewhere else unless Billy Ray agreed to sell by the end of the week. Now it was Wednesday. *He would rather die poor and cost this town its future than share the million dollars with his wife*, people said. *He is one mean SOB.*

So this was a week the town would never forget. In two days, they would lose a chance to make the town rich and famous. At noon, it was struck by the biggest thunderstorm anyone could recall.

And now it had its first-ever murder.

THREE

Max was at home the day Billy Ray was shot. There was always paperwork to be done, and she chose to do it there. She enjoyed the silence and visits with her next-door neighbor Geegee. *It's Gillian with a G,* the woman said when they met. *And Gallup, my husband's last name. So I've been Geegee since we married.* She rolled her eyes. *Twenty-one years ago.* She was a small woman, with short blond hair and a boyish figure.

I'm here all the time, Geegee said. *My husband Cliff's a bigamist. He's married to me and the music store. Gallup Guitars? On the corner near the lake? When he's not selling, he's teaching, and when he's not teaching, he's playing somewhere.* She waved a hand and laughed. *I'm a music widow. Anyway, you want company, I'm here. You want me to watch your place, I'm here for that too.*

Max was pleased to have Geegee as a friend. The truth was, she was glad to have anyone as a friend. The people of Port Ainslie were proud that their town had a woman police chief. But they were not eager to get close to Max. Not right away. She was new to the town, after all. No one was rude to her. They were just not in a hurry to be her friend. Except for Geegee.

So while Max got to know many of the folks in town, she could talk openly only with Geegee.

It will take time, Geegee told her, *but they'll come around.* Meaning the people in and around Port Ainslie. *You'll see. Just keep doing a good job like you are and smiling a lot.*

Max and Geegee were soon sharing stories, over wine for Geegee, coffee for Max. Once or twice Max met Geegee's husband, Cliff. He seemed pleasant, but Max saw a man divided. Cliff had time for his store and time for his music. This did not leave much time for his wife. Geegee, Max thought, needed their friendship as much as Max did.

Max had not been thinking about Cliff Gallup the day Billy Ray was killed. She was lost in planning next year's budget, until a clap of thunder shook the house. She stood at the window for a while to watch storm clouds sweep across the lake toward town. Then she went back to work while the rain pounded on the roof and beat against the windows.

At two thirty the storm had long passed, leaving behind a beautiful day. The air was calm, the sun was shining...and Margie called to tell Max that Billy Ray had been found dead. *I have a report of a body,* she said. *In a garage at 873 Main Street. Wojak is at the site.*

Sounds like Billy Ray's house, Max said. She was out of her chair and on her way to the door.

Why, my word, Margie said. *I do believe it is.*

———

Margie had called Henry after getting the call about Billy Ray being found dead. Henry had been nearby, in his car on Main Street, when the call came in.

When Henry got to Billy Ray's house, he ordered people to stay back from the open garage door. Then he put yellow police tape across the driveway but left the garage door open. Anyone on the street could see Billy Ray's body, and some stood looking at it from the end of the driveway.

This was not the way to do things at a murder scene, and Henry knew it. He wanted the world, or at least people in town, to know what had happened to Billy Ray. It was a bit of revenge for Henry. He didn't like Billy Ray any more than anyone else in town. Henry liked him even less, if that were possible. But he had good reason.

Billy Ray had once tried to charge Henry with police brutality. He said Henry had used too much force when arresting Billy Ray for stealing snow tires. A judge did not agree, and the charge was dropped. But Billy Ray's complaint went into Henry's file. Henry was sure that this black mark on his file kept him from winning the job of police chief. That's why the town council, Henry thought, looked for someone else. They chose Max instead of him. Henry liked Max, but from that day on he hated Billy Ray.

About a dozen people were at the end of Billy Ray's driveway when Max arrived. She checked the time: 2:43 PM. She would put this in her report.

Among the people at the scene were Ivan Curic, Brenda Karp, Seth Torsney, Ben Black and Sam Little. All stood behind the yellow tape Henry had stretched across the driveway. They were staring at Billy Ray's body slumped in a patio chair you could buy at the hardware store for ten dollars.

"Afternoon, Chief," Sam said. He and the others stepped aside to make room for Max.

Max did not answer. Instead, as she walked to the garage she barked, "Keep everybody back." Her eyes were on Billy Ray.

Billy Ray's head was down. His chin was on his chest, and his arms hung at his sides. His eyes were open as though he were staring at his feet. He wore a black T-shirt, cut-off jeans and boots with no socks. A trail of blood led down the back of the chair to the floor of the garage.

Max looked at the scene, soaking up the details. Henry walked into the garage to stand beside her. "When are you going to call the OPP?" he asked.

"Who says I am?" she said.

Henry looked at Max like she had grown a second head. Then he walked back to the people behind the yellow plastic tape.

Max moved to look closely at the body. Billy Ray had been shot in the back of the head while sitting in his garage, facing the closed door. His shotgun lay across his lap on top of an open magazine. A large Tim Hortons coffee cup sat on an old metal table next to him. Also on the table was an open bottle of rum. Billy Ray, Max thought, had been adding courage to his coffee. A box of shotgun shells was at his feet.

Two shells had been taken from the box. Max had no doubt that they were in the shotgun.

She looked around the garage. Was anything out of place? Was there something here that should not be here?

Billy Ray had come and gone from his house through his garage. One of the changes Brenda Karp had helped him make was putting a new steel door in the front entrance. Billy bricked up the back door facing the lake. *Don't want nobody comin' in that way and sneakin' up on me*, he had said. *They come in the front, or they don't come in at all*. Then he put a new steel door on the entrance from the garage.

It's like a trap he never got to set, Brenda Karp had told Max. She meant the house. *You get into the garage easy, but not into the house. He was going to put in a new door, one you could open from the truck. Never got around to it. Didn't even fix the lock on the old garage door. Just kept putting it off. He'd rather ride his Harley-Davidson and drink beer.*

From inside the garage, Max could hear the others talking at the end of the driveway.

Ivan Curic said, "Maybe now we'll get that resort built." When Ivan looked up to see Max glaring at him, Ivan didn't try to hide his smile. All the property for the resort site had been priced by Ivan. The price he gave to the resort company was the offer it had made to every owner. Including Billy Ray.

That's why Billy Ray had let Ivan inspect his property. He wanted to know the price so he could turn it down. Ivan was there long enough to name a price. He told the resort company that Billy Ray's land was worth four hundred thousand dollars. They offered that to Billy Ray, who told them he had let Ivan put a price on his land but had not agreed to sell it. And he would not sell it at any price. *I just wanted to know how much I would turn down*, he said with a laugh. The company raised its price. Billy Ray still said no. Each time he was offered more money, Billy Ray turned it down. All the way up to the final bid of one million dollars.

Max thought about this while she looked at the things inside Billy Ray's garage. She walked to his pickup truck, parked next to his body. A blue plastic sheet covered the truck bed. When Max lifted the sheet and looked in, she saw bags of cedar-mulch nuggets in the truck bed. She lowered the sheet and walked to a work-bench near the motorcycle in the corner. "Did anybody hear a gunshot?" she called out to Henry.

"No one heard a thing," Henry said. He walked toward her. "They all heard the thunderstorm, but nobody heard a gun.

If he was killed in the middle of that storm, nobody could've heard it."

Henry was a sad-faced man. When Max had first met Henry, she'd thought it was because he was unhappy about not being made chief. But she soon learned this had nothing to do with Henry's look. He just had a sad-looking face. She knew about the black mark on his record that Billy Ray had put there. Would this make it a problem to work with Henry now?

"Take this sheet off the truck," she said to Henry, "and cover the body with it. The whole town doesn't have to see what's left of Billy Ray."

When Henry pulled the sheet off the bags of mulch, a loud voice called out, "Well, look at that!"

Max turned to see Seth pointing at Billy Ray's truck. "The guy was a thief," Seth said. He raised his voice louder. "A common thief. He stole those from me last night."

Max walked farther into the garage, headed for an open window at the rear. The window was on the side of the garage away from the house, and its lock was broken. By all the rust on it, she could tell it had been broken for years.

She stood at the window and looked back to the body. With her eyes she drew a straight line from the window to the back of Billy Ray's head. A person standing outside the window would have a clear view of him. Or, more to the point, she thought, a clear shot. She was sure this was where the killer stood and took aim.

She looked out the open window and down at the ground. Someone had torn branches from the high shrubs that blocked a view from the street. They had dropped the branches on the ground under the window. When they stood there, looking at Billy Ray's back, they left no footprints. From there they could have slid the window open and shot Billy Ray. Then they left without leaving a trace. Max was sure that was how Billy Ray had been murdered.

She went back to the body and lifted one of Billy Ray's tattooed arms from under the sheet. She was looking for lividity, a redness in the skin caused when blood settles in a dead body. An expert can tell how long a person has been dead by the lividity. Max looked at Billy Ray's arm and hand. He had, she guessed, been dead for two, maybe three, hours.

Max stepped past Billy Ray to look at the group outside on the driveway. The sun was still shining brightly. She could hear music and laughing children from out on the lake. As she walked out of the garage, the sound of their joy and the view of the dead body gave her chills. So much joy, she thought. And so much sorrow. That's what life was all about.

JOHN LAWRENCE REYNOLDS

"Who found him?" she asked the group behind the yellow tape. None of them seemed upset over Billy Ray's death.

"We all did," said Ivan Curic. "We came down here to have it out with Billy Ray."

"And there he was," Sam Little said. "Deader'n day-old roadkill."

"That's when I called it in to Margie," Ivan said.

"Here comes Ryan," Seth said.

Max turned to see Ryan Kelly jogging from the downtown area.

"I just heard," Ryan said when he reached them. He bent to look past Max at Billy Ray's body. "Is he really dead?"

"He really is," Ben Black said. He and Ryan exchanged high fives.

"Now who would have done a thing like that?" Ryan said with a laugh.

Which made Max snap into action. "You may think this is a joke," she barked, "but I don't. Someone committed murder here.

The dead man may not have been your idea of a saint, but no one has the right to do that. And no one has the right to treat it as a joke!"

The group fell quiet.

Max turned to Henry. "Close that door and seal it with tape," she ordered. "This is now a crime scene." She looked back to the crowd on the driveway. "Anyone who goes into that garage will be arrested." She looked at Henry again. "Call the morgue in Cranston," she said just as loudly. "Tell the coroner we have a body to be looked at and taken for an autopsy. Stay here until he comes. Tell him I want to hear his first opinion right away. Have him call me as soon as he can."

"Do I call the OPP too?" Henry said.

She glared at him. "Did I tell you to?"

Henry jerked his head like he had been slapped.

She turned back to the onlookers. No one was laughing now. "I want all of you who were here when the body was found to meet me in my office at four o'clock sharp," she said. "That means you too, Ryan. And I don't want any of you to talk about this. Not among yourselves, and not to anyone else. Not a word."

She looked them all straight in the eye: Ivan Curic, Sam Little, Brenda Karp, Seth Torsney, Ben Black and Ryan Kelly. "Anyone who talks about this, or who is a minute late to my office, will be subject to arrest." Walking to the cruiser she heard Ben say, "Can she really arrest us for that?"

"You're darn right I can," she said over her shoulder. "And I *will!*"

First rule of being in charge, Max thought as she drove away, is to act like you are.

And she had.

FOUR

It worked. When Max stepped out of her office at four o'clock, all six were in the station boardroom. They were drinking coffee and talking. Henry stood to one side of the door with his natural sad face. He was trying to look and sound like a tough cop. It was not working.

"They're in there telling stories like it's a party," Margie said. "You would think they would behave better since someone was murdered."

"It depends on who was murdered," Max said.

Margie paused on her way to her desk. "You know," she said, "I have been thinking. I could not warm to Billy Ray. No more than anyone else in town. But I remember when he was a little boy in short pants. He was a cutie-pie back then. Maybe his adult version wasn't. But whoever shot the grown-up jerk also shot the little boy too. Don't you think?"

Max nodded as Margie went to the kitchen to make more coffee. Margie Burns, Max thought, might be the smartest person in Port Ainslie.

The coroner had called to say Billy Ray had been shot with a small-caliber weapon. He guessed it was a .22. The killer had fired the gun through the open window at the back of the garage. It happened, he guessed, at noon or a short time thereafter. Billy Ray's body was now on its way to Cranston for a full autopsy.

It was just as Max had thought.

"Which of you own a .22 rifle?" she said as she walked into the boardroom.

Ben and Ryan raised their hands. Many people kept a .22 rifle to shoot rats or raccoons. Some went target shooting in an old quarry down the road. A few owned guns because their fathers had. Rifles were handed down to children like watches and earrings, family heirlooms.

Ben turned to Sam and said, "You got a .22."

Sam said, "Yeah, but it's a pistol, not a rifle."

Max thought about that. Then she said, "Here's what we're going to do. I will talk to you in my office, one at a time. Except for you, Brenda and Seth. I'll talk with you together. Henry will stay here and make sure none of you leave the building until I say you can go. Margie will keep the coffee pot full for you. Anyone have a problem with that?"

Ryan and Ben said they were needed at their businesses. Ryan ran a small vineyard down the lake and sold wine through a retail store on Main Street. "I need to be in the store," he said. "This will cost me money."

Ben was a plumber, the only one in town. He was always busy at this time of year. "I got two service calls to make today," he said.

"I'll talk to you first," Max said to Ben. "In about ten minutes. With luck, you will all be gone in an hour." She started walking back to her office. Then she stopped and said, "Maybe all but one of you." Looking at Brenda and Seth, she added, "Or maybe two." She winked at Margie.

She couldn't resist it.

———

Max needed time to think about the questions she would ask. She was sure the murderer was among those in the board-room. Whoever had shot Billy Ray knew he would be sitting in his garage. The murderer, of course, would need a motive to kill him in the first place. In that case, every person waiting in the boardroom could be a suspect.

As she wrote their names on a lined paper pad, Max felt proud and tense. She was proud of the things she had done with her life so far. She had come second in her class at the police academy and made first-class constable within two years. Twice she had been named Officer of the Month by the Toronto police force. She had two medals for bravery and one for taking top place in target shooting. That one made her extra proud, because she hated guns.

She had achieved all of these things even though everyone called her Max. No one called her Maxine or even Mrs. Benson when she was married. It was always Max.

Why couldn't she have a nice name like Anne or Faith or Jennifer? Maybe one of those old names that were in style again. Like Sophia or Emma or Abigail. She liked Abigail. If she were Abigail, she wouldn't mind being called Abby. Abby sounded like a nice person, and Max had always thought of herself that way. Abby was a person. Max? Max was still a truck driver's name, and always would be to her.

She had tried not to let it bother her, but it still did. She just would not let others know. All through her career as a police officer, not once had she complained about being called Max. It was her way to prove she could handle anything. Even a name she hated.

Her first name was no fault of her own, but she took the blame for marrying Brian Benson. Brian had been a tough cop and a rotten husband. When their marriage ended, she felt all kinds of emotions.

Some were sad and filled with regret. Most were happy and filled with relief. And there was some pride too. If you didn't count her failed marriage, she had reached all the goals she had set for life as a police officer.

Except one. The one that was making her tense.

She had never solved a murder on her own.

She was about to fix that, she told herself, in the next few hours.

———

Ben Black was admired by almost everyone in town. With his thick, dark hair, quick smile and plumbing skills, Ben was both busy and popular. He smiled when he came into the room, wearing old jeans and heavy boots. Max noticed his hands were greasy. He sat in a chair across from her desk.

"Where were you this morning?" she asked Ben.

Ben looked away. Then he said, "I went to see Billy Ray."

"At what time?" Max asked. She was making notes.

"I'm guessing about noon."

"Don't guess," Max said. "I want to hear the exact time, if you can give it."

Ben looked at the ceiling, then nodded. "It was noon. Right in the middle of that storm. Maybe five minutes after twelve, no more. I was heading west of town. Had a call to be there between twelve thirty and one. Gave me time to stop and talk to that son of...to talk to Billy Ray."

"What about?"

Ben's mood changed, and Max saw anger in his eyes. "About the five hundred dollars he owes me for putting in a new tub. He'd promised to pay me today. He'd been promising to pay me for months. I went to collect it, and I started to open Billy Ray's garage door. That's how you got into his house, through the garage. When I went to lift the door I heard him say, *Open it and you're dead*. I dropped the door real quick when I heard that."

"Do you think he was serious?" Max asked.

Ben shook his head. "You never could tell with Billy Ray," he said. "He sounded like he meant it. I asked when I would get my money, and he said when he was good and ready. I asked him when that would be, and he said, *How about when hell freezes over?* I'm standing there in the rain and the thunder and all. There was no arguing with Billy Ray. Figured I'd get going and come back some other time. I called him a few names, then ran back to my truck and drove off."

"Where's your rifle?"

"Loaned it to Seth last week. He and Brenda wanted to go shoot some targets in the quarry."

Max made more notes. Then she said, "Go wait in the other room, and tell Seth and Brenda to come in."

Seth Torsney and Brenda Karp came into Max's office holding hands. Brenda wore a cotton top that was too low and too tight. Her jeans looked like they had been painted on her very long, very slim legs. Her blond hair was pulled back with a pink ribbon, and her eyes shone a deep blue. Max felt a hint of jealousy. Seth wore faded khakis and a T-shirt printed with the name of his business: *Torsney's Garden Grove*.

"Which one of you lovebirds shot Billy Ray?" Max asked when they were seated in their chairs.

Both looked shocked. Together they said, "Not me!" and Brenda added, "You're kidding, right?"

Max said, "I never kid." But she liked to catch people off guard. Then she said, "Where were you two this morning?"

They looked at each other and blushed. "We kind of slept in," Seth said.

Brenda said, "We fooled around some in bed," and Seth laughed and said, "Some?"

"Hey!" Max was almost shouting. "We're dealing with a murder here, damn it."

Her voice was loud enough to make the couple stop laughing and change their expressions. Brenda bit her lip. Seth nodded to say he understood.

"You two had better start getting serious," Max said. "I don't need a picture of your morning antics. Just tell me the time you got up. I don't care what you were doing before then. I only care what you were doing after. So. What time was it when you got out of bed?"

"About nine or nine thirty," Brenda said.

"Then what?" Max asked.

"I drove to work in my truck," Seth said. "See, the reason I got up was one of my guys called to say we'd been robbed. I wasn't going to go in until noon, but…" He shrugged his shoulders.

"You thought it was Billy Ray," Max said.

Seth nodded. "The stuff you saw in Billy Ray's truck? That's it. That's the kind I sell. I figured it was him soon as I heard about it. He's taken stuff from me before at night. I just couldn't prove it was him. About fifty bags of cedar garden nuggets. Worth four or five hundred dollars. That's what was gone, and that's what was on his truck."

"What would he do with the mulch?"

"Sell it for half price."

"Who would he sell it to?"

"Gardeners, other nurseries. Anybody looking to save a few bucks. He'd wink and tell them it fell off a truck. You know what I think? I think he stole from me because of Brenda. He thought I stole her from him, so he'd steal from me."

Max thought about this. Then she said, "What time was it when you got to work and learned what had been stolen?"

"About ten. As I said, I was going to take the morning off, but…"

Brenda took over. "You would not believe what they steal from us at night," she said. "You just can't trust people…"

Max held up a hand and said, "Do I smell cedar?"

Seth brought a hand to his nose and nodded. "Sell a lot of young cedar trees this time of year," he said.

"He comes home some nights, he smells like a whole forest," Brenda said.

Max turned to Brenda. "How about you?" she said. "Where were you this morning?"

"Well, I did some laundry..." Brenda said.

"Change the bedsheets?"

Brenda blushed. "I made some lunch and took it to Seth around noon. We ate sandwiches together at the nursery. I wanted to go and ask Billy Ray for my jewelry one more time. I took Seth's truck and headed up to his house just as the storm arrived."

"And what time was that?"

"About twenty after twelve."

"I didn't want her to go," Seth said. "I didn't want her near that guy."

Max turned to Brenda. "So why did you go?"

"I wanted to get my mother's rings back. I was going to tell him to keep the other stuff. Just let me have Mom's rings." Brenda's eyes filled with tears. "That's all I wanted from him." She wiped her eyes with the back of her hand. Seth reached out to rub her back. She leaned on his shoulder and said, "I never got there. To Billy Ray's. Not before I heard he was dead."

"Why not?" Max said.

"I met Sammy Little on Main Street. He was coming the other way, toward me. When I waved at him, he stopped his truck and rolled down the window to ask where I was going. We could hardly hear each other with the rain and all. I told him, and he said I should stay away from Billy Ray's, and that someone should call the police. He said, *Ol' Billy Ray's in there with a loaded shotgun. Somebody should get that lady cop to go in and take that gun from him.* That's what he told me."

"Why didn't you or Sammy call me?"

"I thought somebody else might do it. I lost my nerve about going to Billy Ray's place after hearing about him with a loaded gun. We were in front of Suzie's dress shop, Sammy and I, and I saw she had put up her summer-sale signs. So I parked the truck to wait for the storm to pass and maybe go shopping."

"That's when you called me," Seth said.

"That's right," Brenda said. "I called Seth on my cell phone to tell him what I was doing. I told him what Sam Little had said. Then I said maybe we should call Ivan and tell him about Billy Ray..."

"Why call Ivan?" Max said. "Why not call me, like Sam said?"

Brenda shrugged. "He seemed to..." She wiped her eyes again and started over. "Ivan knows Billy Ray as well as anybody and..." She seemed unable to go on.

And he's a man, Max thought. Not a woman police chief.

"It was my idea to call him," Seth said. "I was fed up with Billy Ray, and now he was threatening people with a shotgun. I figured Ivan would call you and Henry to deal with the gun. Thought it would be best if we all said you should do something about it. Anyway, Ivan said we should form a group to meet Billy Ray and talk to him about the resort."

"I thought it was a dumb idea," Brenda said. "I told Seth that Billy Ray won't go along with anybody but himself."

"What do you know about the sliding window?" Max said to her.

"Window?" Brenda asked.

"At the back of the garage. You lived there with him. Did he keep that window shut?"

"Sometimes," Brenda said. "But he couldn't lock it. I know that lock didn't work. I told him over and over, *You should fix the lock on that window. Someone can slide it open and get in the garage.* Billy Ray said it wouldn't matter. He said you just need to turn the handle on the garage door to open it. No need to crawl through the window. I kept telling him until he said

I was nagging him and that I'd better stop it. So I did."

"Why was the garage door not locked?" Max asked.

Brenda smiled. "Billy Ray was good at putting in new stuff, but he didn't like to fix what was already there. He'd buy new things but wouldn't fix old stuff."

Max turned to Seth and said, "Where is Ben's rifle?"

Seth sat back in his chair. Caught him, Max thought. "How do you know...?" Seth said.

Max said, "Just tell me where it is."

"In our upstairs closet."

"When was the last time you used it?"

"Last night," Brenda said. "Seth took me to the quarry out near the Point. He showed me how to use it, and we shot at some old tin cans we took with us. It was the first time I ever shot a gun."

"She was good too," Seth said. "For a woman." He reached to squeeze her arm, and Brenda leaned toward him.

"Seth should know," Brenda said. "He won a prize for shooting when he was in the army. Didn't you, Seth?"

Seth smiled and said, "A few."

Max might have told Seth that she had won her own share of shooting awards with the police force, but she was too busy writing notes. When she finished she said, "Have Margie send in Ivan Curic."

FIVE

Ivan Curic wore a linen jacket over an open-collared white shirt. He smiled across the desk at Max and said, "I didn't want things to end this way. Billy Ray tried to stop the best thing that could happen to this town, but he did not deserve to be shot like that. No sir."

"Where were you this morning?" Max asked.

Ivan squinted his eyes and said, "Let's see. I showed a house on Maple Street and got my ad ready for next week's paper. Then I went to check out some land near Rockcliffe Point."

"Rockcliffe Point?" Max said. "Why did you go there?"

"For the resort company. In case Billy Ray still wouldn't sell. If that was the case, I would show them Rockcliffe Point and give them a plan B."

"I thought the resort had to be built on Billy Ray's land or nowhere," Max said.

"You never know," Ivan said. "You gotta be ready for change in this business. That's how you make it big. You always have a plan B in your pocket."

"How much of this resort deal are you a part of?"

Ivan sat and thought a bit. "I'm not in on the action, if that's what you mean. I'm just trying to help the company. Of course, I plan to buy some land of my own before it's built. The resort, I mean. Everybody should. Land values will shoot through the roof here. The resort is just the beginning. It will bring new business, new people moving in. You mark my words. Lots of people are going to get rich from it."

"People like you."

"I hope so. But it won't be just me. This kind of thing can help all of us."

"Tell me about the land you went to look at today."

"I got out of town just when that storm broke. Now *that* was a storm, wasn't it? I haven't seen one like that since I was a kid. The rain was so heavy, I had to pull over to the side of the road until it stopped. When it let up I started to drive again. I passed Henry on his way into town and honked at him. I guess he didn't see me, because he kept going."

"What time was that?" Max asked.

"I'm guessing twelve, maybe twelve thirty," Ivan said. "Like I said, the rain had let up some. So I went to look at a place down the lake. Then, on the way back, I thought about Billy Ray and what he was doing to this town. It made me darn mad. Soon's I got to my office I got a call from Seth, who gave me an idea. Maybe we should all go and talk to Billy Ray together. At least we could say we tried. So I started calling people who I knew were fed up with him and his tricks. I called Ben, Ryan and Sam. Seth and Brenda were already in. I said that we should do what good citizens always do. And that's try and settle things ourselves instead of bothering Chief Benson about it."

Ivan watched Max, waiting for a smile of thanks for calling her Chief. When he didn't get one, he went back to talking.

"We decided to let Billy Ray know how we felt about what he was doing to the town," Ivan said.

"You own a .22?" Max asked.

"Used to. Had it stolen during all those break-ins a couple of years ago."

"Did you report the theft?"

Ivan shook his head. "The gun was old, not worth much. It had been my dad's. Can't remember the last time I shot it."

"Where did you go to look at land for the resort?"

"I told you. Down the lake at the Point." He waved to the east. "Just to have a plan B in hand."

———

Max sent Ivan back to the others. Then she called Henry Wojak to her office. "Were you out near the Point today?" she asked.

"Cruised out that way before noon," he said. "Just checking things out. That storm hit on the way back to town. Got so bad I pulled over to wait it out. Kept the radio on in case I got a call. But I didn't."

"You see anybody in your travels?"

Henry nodded. "Passed Billy Ray leaving Tim Hortons. Darn fool drove right through the storm."

"Notice anything else?"

"Sammy Little was there at Tim Hortons. Saw his truck outside. And Ryan Kelly. His fancy sports car was parked there too."

Max said, "Send Kelly in."

———

Ryan Kelly made sure everyone in town knew how much he gave up to move to Port Ainslie and start his career as a winemaker. He had been a stock trader in Toronto with a big house in town and a farm in the country. His wife had been a top fashion model. He gave it up, he told everyone, to buy land north of town and grow grapes for wine.

As much as he liked the idea, his wife did not. In fact, she hated it, and they soon divorced. That was five years ago. Since then Ryan seemed to be making a success of his winery. People who knew about such things said his wines were sure to become famous in a few years.

His wines might have been doing well, but Kelly had spent a lot of money to get where he was. Most of the money to start the winery had been borrowed. It was an open secret that Chateau Milford Wines was deeply in debt. Someday the wines might make Kelly rich, but that day was years away. Until then, Kelly's bank and friends who had loaned him cash owned more of his winery than he did.

None of this seemed to bother Kelly. At forty-four years of age, he drove an expensive sports car around town and lived well. To the people in small-town Port Ainslie, he was a very calm and cool guy. Until now. Sitting across from Max, he did not look calm and cool. He looked nervous and upset.

"Where were you this morning?" Max asked Kelly when he sat down.

"Let me see," Kelly said. He looked at the ceiling as he spoke. "I opened the shop at nine and set up some wines for tasting.

I talked with the staff and set up displays. Then I went for a drive."

"A drive?"

"It was a nice day. Before the storm hit."

"What time did you leave the store?"

"Half an hour before noon. Maybe more."

"Where did you drive to?"

"Tim Hortons on the highway."

"Why?"

It was a simple question, but Kelly looked as though it was a hard one to answer. "I bought some coffee and a box of donuts." He shifted in his chair. "The strange thing is…" He hesitated. Then he said, "Billy Ray was there. He was getting ready to leave just as I arrived. Left in the middle of that storm. He didn't care. He never cared about anything."

"Did you two talk?" Max said.

"I asked if he had changed his mind and might sell his land," Kelly said. "He said, *Hell, no. And nobody's making me. I'm going back to sit in the garage with my shotgun as long as it takes. Nobody's getting my land, at any price.* He had an extra-large coffee with him. He said he would stay there until the people who wanted his land gave up trying. He said they could take their big plans somewhere else. I believed him. I met Sam Little inside the shop and told him what Billy Ray had told me. I said Sammy should tell Henry or you that Billy Ray might do something dumb."

"Where did you go with your coffee and donuts?"

Max liked to ask questions from out of nowhere. Sometimes you got an answer you didn't expect. Like this time.

Kelly thought for a moment. Then he said, "Down the lake a mile or two."

"Which way?"

"Pardon?"

Max bit off each word. "Which way did you go with your donuts and coffee?"

"East," he said. "I went east."

"To Rockcliffe Point?"

Kelly looked surprised. "Yes...Yes, down that way."

Max asked whom the coffee and donuts were for.

Sweat showed on Ryan's brow. "A friend."

"Who is she?"

Ryan grew tense. "She's, uh..."

"Married?"

"No...not quite."

"What does that mean?"

"She is kind of married, but she lives alone..."

"Deborah Edwards? Billy Ray's soon-to-be-ex-wife? Is that where you went with coffee, donuts and...?" She left other words hanging in the air and waited for Ryan to speak.

Ryan bit his lower lip. He slumped in his chair.

"Look, Ryan," Max said. "If you want to fool with someone's wife, that is your business. I don't care. Just tell me the truth."

Kelly nodded to her.

"So you have donuts and coffee with the soon-to-be-ex-Mrs. Billy Ray Edwards," Max said. "Then what?"

Kelly folded his hands in his lap and sat up straight. "I came back through town on my way to the vineyard. I wanted to check on the vines after the storm. I was worried it might have damaged the crop. Ivan called me at the vineyard and said I should come back to town. He said we would all meet to talk about Billy Ray and what to do with him."

"And you went to meet with them?"

"Yes."

"What time did you get there?"

"Sometime after two. They had started talking by the time I arrived."

"What about?"

"They agreed that Billy Ray would spoil things for the town. Ivan said we should have it out with that rascal right now. That's how he put it. *We should all go down there now and have it out with him. Talk to him all together. Who will come with me?* I said I would go, but first I had to do some work at the store. I needed to check the stock, that sort of thing. So I said I would meet them all at Billy Ray's. I spent more time at the store than I thought I would. When I got to Billy Ray's, I met you there."

Max stared at Ryan. Had Billy Ray been jealous about Deborah, even more than a year after she left him? How would Billy Ray have felt about her and Ryan mixed up in a romance? She wanted to think about that. For now, she had heard all she needed to hear from Ryan Kelly. "Tell Margie to send in Sam Little," she said. "And go have a strong coffee. You look like you could use one."

SIX

Sam Little could fix a leaky roof, weld a bed frame or paint a house. He did good work for not much money. He also spent as much time trading gossip as he did working on the job at hand. Now he sat in Max's office, wearing a blue shirt and jeans with a red kerchief around his neck. His long gray hair was tied back in a ponytail. He looked like Willie Nelson's younger brother.

"Let's see," Sam said when Max asked where he had been that day. "I read the paper at Tim Hortons…"

"Is that where you met Ryan Kelly?"

"That's right," Sam said. "Saw Billy Ray there too. Saw him talk to Ryan a bit. When Billy Ray left, Ryan came and told me Billy Ray had a gun. Said he might use it. Said I should tell you or Henry."

"And did you?"

"I told Henry. See, I left just as that storm hit. Boy, that was something, wasn't it? I stopped the truck under a bridge when the rain came down hard. When it was over I saw Henry coming. I waved him down and told him what Ryan Kelly had told me. I said maybe one of you should go to Billy Ray and get him to see some reason."

"What did Henry say?"

"He said he would look into it."

"What next?"

"I went home to start putting down new floor tile. The wife has been at me for weeks to get it done. Then Ivan called to say there was a meeting at his office.

Said I should come and help decide what to do about Billy Ray."

"Did you go?"

"Sure did. I was glad to go. Hate doing tile. Down on your knees all day—"

"Just tell me what went on at the meeting," Max said.

"Well, when I got there I told Ivan what I had heard from Ryan. That's when things got started. We all agreed we had to do something. I mean, short of murder, right? Nobody talked about that. Next thing I know we're walking the couple of blocks down Main Street to Billy Ray's. When we got there, Ivan is so worked up he lifts the garage door before anybody can say anything. And there he is. Billy Ray, I mean. We knew he was dead as soon as we saw him."

Max told Sam to go back to the boardroom and to stay with the others until she said they could leave. As he was about to go out the door, she said, "How well do you know Deborah Edwards?"

Sam turned back to smile at her. "Not near as well as I'd like to."

———

When Sam left, Max called Henry Wojak to her office. "Did Sam Little tell you Billy Ray was in his garage with a loaded gun on his lap?" she said.

Henry thought, then said, "Yes, he did."

"And did Sam think one of us should go and talk some sense into him?"

"Uh-huh," Henry said. "He said that too."

"What did you do about it?"

"Nothing."

"Why?"

"Thought it might be best for you to do it."

Max sat for a time and stared at Henry. "Why would you want me to face Billy Ray?" she said.

Henry looked edgy. "I thought he'd listen to you," he said. "Never listened to me. Never paid me any mind."

"But you didn't tell me, did you?"

Henry look down and nodded. "Forgot all about it after we found him dead. Thing like that can shake you up. Kinda wipe your mind clean. If you know what I mean."

Max stared at him a moment longer. Then she said, "Tell them all I'll be there in a minute," she said.

When Henry left, Max looked at her notes. The key was there. One of the people she had just talked to had shot Billy Ray. She knew it.

All of them had a reason to do it. And each had a chance. It would take less than a minute to walk to the window at the rear of the garage. Rip some branches off a cedar tree and drop them on the ground. Lean through the window, take aim, and shoot Billy Ray from behind. Then go.

If it was still storming, nobody would be around to see you. And no one would hear the shot with all the rain and thunder.

They would not have a problem with a gun. Guns were as common as crows in the area. Folks didn't keep track of all the guns they had. You could buy a .22 rifle in these parts and nobody would know you had it.

Were they all part of a plot to kill Billy Ray? Max thought about that, but it didn't make sense. They had all moved around too much when the storm hit, when Billy Ray had been shot. No, she told herself, Billy Ray had been killed by one person. Two at the most.

Something someone had said in the past half hour told her who had done it. She was sure of that. She just had to figure out what it was and who had said it.

Max sat and read over her notes a second time. Then a third time. Where was it? *What* was it? She wondered if one of the hotshots at the would spot it. If they did and named the killer right away, would they tease her about it? Would they say small-town cops like her should leave murder to them? Of course they would. She hated the idea. But she had to be honest. She was a good cop, and good cops get help when they need it. It did not make sense to stay stubborn and pig-headed. Like Billy Ray had been. She should swallow her pride and turn everything over to the OPP.

She sighed, knowing she would have to call the OPP. If she could not solve the crime before they arrived, she could at least build a thick file of clues for them.

She could hear Ivan Curic's voice through her open door. He was speaking to everyone in the boardroom, and she went to hear what he was telling them.

Ivan's back was to her when she entered the room. "I'll treat us all to coffee, snacks and maybe some of Ryan Kelly's wine," he was saying. Margie was near the window with her arms folded, looking bored. Henry was leaning against a wall. "We can get a lot done now that—"

"Now that what?" Max said.

Ivan turned and tried to smile. "I was just saying now that..." He stopped to think of the next word to say.

"Now that Billy Ray is no longer alive?" Max said.

"Well, look," Ivan said.

"Ivan means that we can get some things done now," Ryan said. He was more cool than when he had spoken to Max in her office. "We can meet tonight and talk about how to get that resort built."

"That's right," Seth said. "It's too bad, Billy Ray being shot and all, but that's how things go. Those folks in Toronto, the money people, they can go to Billy Ray's wife. When they get her on their side, we'll be on our way."

"Maybe she won't sell," Ben said. "Maybe she'll be like Billy Ray. Do you think so?" He looked at Ivan.

"I'll talk to the resort folk, tell them about Billy Ray and that we hear his wife will get the land," Ivan said. "My guess is, they'll wait for the will to be settled. And I'm betting that his wife will sign for a million cash. Who wouldn't?" He turned to Max. "What do you think?" he asked.

"None of my business," Max said. "What time is this meeting you're talking about?"

"Eight o'clock," Ivan said. "At my office. You're welcome to come. The whole town is welcome. You come by and I'll save a coffee and butter tart for you."

"Forget the coffee and tart," Max said. She turned to leave and got the keys to the new cruiser. "But I will be there." She stopped to look back at them. "I want all of you there too," she said. Then she asked Margie to come to her office.

"Call the provincials in Cranston," she said. "Tell them to bring their homicide team. I'm on my way east to the Point." Walking to the door she said, "Keep an eye on things while I'm gone." Then she added in a lower voice, "Including Henry."

SEVEN

Rockcliffe Point was just a mile east of Port Ainslie, but it was not at all like the rest of the area. West of town, the lakeshore was all wide beaches of soft white sand. The land to the east was bare and rocky, squeezed between the lake and Granite Mountain. When heavy snow fell, the Point could be cut off from the rest of the town for days. And the wind that blew down from the mountain could be cold and raw.

Max looked around as she drove along the road to the Point. She was glad she had chosen to live west of town, where the air was soft and the breezes were gentle.

Only a few cottages were at Rockcliffe Point, and she found Deborah Edwards's without a problem. Like others on the road, it sat among thin trees that clung to the poor soil. A gray cedar-shake roof, with a large stone chimney poking out of it, topped dull-brown siding. Two large windows looked out onto the lake.

Just as Max stepped out of the car, her radio buzzed and she heard Margie say, "You there, Chief?"

Max pressed the mic. "What's up, Marge?" she said. She saw a curtain move at a window of the cottage.

"You're on your own for a while," Margie said. "Just heard from the OPP. That darn bridge is stuck up in the air again. The OPP can't get here for three, maybe four, hours. And get this. The med officer is stuck on this side of the river with Billy Ray's corpse growing cold in the back of his van. Or maybe it's growing warm…"

"Thanks, Margie," Max said. "I'll go in and talk to Mrs. Edwards now. Will call back when I've left."

Max climbed the steps on the lake side of the cottage. Just as she got to the top step the door swung open, and Deborah Edwards stood staring at her. The woman's face was as blank as a dinner plate.

"If you've come to tell me about Billy Ray," Deborah said, "I already know."

Deborah Edwards carried herself as though she had not been called Debbie since she was a child. Some women have that look, Max thought, a look that made you call them by their full names. They were always Deborah, never Debbie. Always Susan, never Sue. Always Judith, never Judy. So why was she always Max and never Maxine?

The woman's high cheekbones and slanted dark eyes gave her a catlike look. She wore a blue cotton sweater with loose threads, old jeans, and sneakers.

"May I ask how you knew about your husband's death?" Max said.

"A friend called me." Deborah did not invite Max inside. In fact, it was clear that she did not want Max there at all.

"When?"

"I don't know. Three this afternoon. Around that time."

Max had a good idea who the friend was. "I would like to talk to you about your husband's death," she said. "May I come in?"

"Sure." Deborah turned and walked into the cottage, leaving Max to close the door herself.

The few pieces of furniture were of good quality, but they had seen better days. Deborah sat in a pine rocker. Max chose a sofa facing a window with a view of the lake. Opening her notebook, she said, "Do you have any idea who might have killed your husband?"

"Just about everyone in town," Deborah said. Did she hide a smile when she said it? Max thought so. This was not a weeping widow. "Except me. I might have, but I couldn't. I've been here all day."

"Alone?"

The smile was gone. "What difference does that make?"

"If you had a visitor it would confirm your alibi."

"I did. Have a visitor."

"Who was that?"

"I'm not sure I have to tell you."

Max turned to look into the kitchen. "Any donuts left?"

Deborah stayed cool. "Sure. You want one? I think some are left over. Take them. If you want more, I can call Ryan."

"Look," Max said. "I know you are not crying over your husband's death, and I know why. We all know why. But I have a job to do, and I can use your help. If you prefer not to help me, I can ask the OPP to take you to Cranston. They'll ask you a lot of stuff there, for a long time. It's up to you. I know Ryan Kelly was here this morning because he told me. He told me a lot of things. And I don't care if you two spent the time in bed or sat at the window and watched birds. I just want you to tell me what time he came here and when he left."

Deborah looked out the window as she spoke. "He got here at noon. He left a little after one. We drank coffee and ate donuts. The rest of the time we did not watch birds. The truth is that we spent most of the time in bed. It was fun."

"You're sure about those times?"

"Yes." Deborah's eyes moved up the wall next to Max. "A little bird told me. The one in that clock. That's the only one we watched." Max turned to see a cuckoo clock on the wall above her head. "It came out at twelve thirty when I was in the kitchen making Ryan some fresh coffee. I brought it to him. In bed." She looked at Max, tilted her head and smiled.

The times matched Ryan Kelly's story. Which didn't make it true, Max told herself. "Tell me, woman to woman," Max said. "What did Billy Ray have that could attract a woman like you, and Brenda Karp, to him?"

Deborah smiled. "Some of us like bad boys. The kind who take you for rides on their motorcycle at night and dare you to do things you don't want to do. They make you feel alive for a while. Maybe you even marry them. Then one day you ask yourself, *What have I done?*" She turned her head to look away. "You either get it or you don't."

Max didn't get it. She had spent years in Toronto around so-called bad boys who had done bad things. She had never seen anything about them that might attract her. But who knew?

Deborah spoke again. "By the way," she said, "I get Billy Ray's house and land. That was my idea. He wanted me, he had to share the land." She tilted her head and smiled again. "No fool here, right? The company that wants to build that resort can have it for one million dollars cash." She held the same cold smile. "In case you didn't know. The price, I mean."

"You sound sure about getting his land," Max said.

"I called the lawyer as soon as I heard. About him being dead, I mean. The land is in both our names, which leaves me the sole owner. We signed a deal that will hold up in court. That gives me a motive, right? To kill him, I mean. But I didn't."

There was nothing more to learn here. Max stood and walked to the door. "Thanks for your time," she said.

"Sure." Deborah was behind her.

At the door, Max looked across the rocks to the lake. "Did you see anybody else here today?" she said.

Deborah did not speak for a moment. Then she said, "When I came to the kitchen for the coffee around twelve thirty. Looked out the window and saw a man from town on the shore over there."

"Did you know him?" Max asked.

"I think it was Ivan, the real-estate guy."

"Ivan Curic? Did you tell Ryan about it?"

She shrugged. "Don't think so. Why bother? He was just walking back to his car, parked on the road. At least he wasn't shooting any guns."

Max turned to her. "What does that mean?"

"That blond piece of fluff Brenda, who moved in with Billy Ray after I left? She and some guy were here last night, in the old quarry past the trees. I could hear them shooting for at least an hour."

"It couldn't have been that loud."

"No, but it made me nervous. I was going to call you and say you should tell them to stop. Then it stopped, so I didn't call. I went out back, and I saw them drive past in her new boyfriend's truck. I stood glaring at them, but they didn't see me. That's it. You on your way now?"

Max walked down the stairs and sat behind the wheel of the police car for a minute. It had been a waste of time and gas to come out here, she thought. There had been nothing to learn from Billy Ray's widow. Ivan Curic had told Max he came to look at the land after the storm passed, and Deborah Edwards said it was true.

Max had to admit the truth. The case would be turned over to the OPP after all. Somewhere in her notes was a clue that would reveal the murderer, but she would have to leave it to the OPP to find it. And accept that when it came to solving a murder, she was in over her head.

But on the way back to town, thinking about the case, it all came to her.

She had found more than a clue to the death of Billy Ray.

She had found the murderer.

EIGHT

"They say the bridge won't be fixed until after seven o'clock," Margie Burns said when Max walked into the police station. It was just after five. "Nobody else called. Henry's gone home to feed his cat. If it's all right with you, I'm going home to make peach jam."

"Can you wait a bit?" Max said. She swept past Margie on the way to her office. "I could use you and Henry to help me tonight."

"With what?"

"An arrest."

Margie's eyes grew wide. "For Billy Ray's murder?"

"That's right." Max entered her office, Margie trotting behind her. "But not until eight o'clock. In the meantime, I want you to make a phone call, then stay and help us if you can."

"The peaches can wait," Margie said. "But I could go home and get some lasagna from the fridge and bring it back for us to eat."

"Good." Max's mind wasn't on lasagna. It was on murder. "Make the phone call first. Bring some food for Henry. Call and tell him to forget the cat and get here right away."

Ivan Curic's office was on the ground floor of the Ainslie Building. Designed by a famous Toronto architect and made of local granite, it was the most stylish building in town. At three stories, it was also the tallest.

Curic Realty was on the building's ground floor. The two floors above it were filled with offices for lawyers, dentists and doctors. At this hour, all were empty except Curic Realty. That office was brightly lit, as though a party was being held there. In a way it was. One desk held bottles of wine and soft drinks. Bowls filled with potato chips and snacks were placed on other desks all around the office. Country music filled the air from large speakers in a corner.

Everyone had changed into better clothes than they had worn that afternoon when they saw Billy Ray's body. Brenda Karp wore a skirt and blouse, and even Ben Black had changed into trousers and a shirt and tie. Most of them sipped from glasses of wine and smiled as they talked, as though they were at a social event. Which they were, even if the event marked someone's death.

"Come in, come in," Ivan called out when he saw Max at the front door. The smile faded when he saw the expression on Max's face. It vanished when Henry Wojak and Margie Burns followed Max into the room. "Is something wrong?" Ivan said.

"Turn the music down," Max said.

Ivan went into his office, and the music stopped.

"Quite a party you have here," Max said when Ivan came back. Henry walked to the rear of the office. Margie stayed near the front door.

"It's not what you think," Ivan said. "We're here to make plans for the town's future."

"What I'm going to do for the town's future," Max said, "is charge someone with Billy Ray's murder."

Brenda was the first to speak. "You think..." Her voice broke, and she had to start over. "You think one of *us* shot Billy Ray?"

"I know it, and I can prove it," Max said.

"Who would do a thing like that?" Seth Torsney said. He moved closer to Brenda and put a hand on her arm.

"Well, you two for a start," Max said.

Brenda began to cry. "You believe…you *really* believe that Seth and I could *do* such a thing?"

"You had some practice with a gun last night, right?" Max said. "Out near Rockcliffe Point."

"Now hold on there," Seth said.

"I won't hold on a minute more than I need to," Max said. She looked at the wall clock. It read *8:20*. She was right on time. Before Seth could speak, she pointed at Ryan Kelly. "You were at Rockcliffe Point today as well, weren't you?" she said.

Ryan stayed calm. "If you think you're spreading gossip," he said, "you're too late. I've told everyone here about Deborah and me."

"How much will it help your business?" Max said.

Ryan said with a frown, "How much will *what* help my business?"

"The million dollars Deborah gets when she sells Billy Ray's land."

"It will be hers to sell, if she wants."

"And yours to use. To save your winery, right?"

"If you're saying…" Ryan began.

Max held a hand up to silence him and turned to Ben. "You were the last person to speak to Billy Ray, weren't you?" she said.

Ben set his glass of red wine on a desk. Then he leaned on it and said, "Yeah. Through a closed door."

"But you were there to get money that Billy Ray owed you, right?"

"So what?"

"Billy Ray said he had a shotgun."

"I told you from the start."

"Which he said he would use."

"I told you that too."

"Which was a good reason for you not to open the door."

"A darn good one."

"If you did, Billy Ray might have shot both barrels of his gun at you."

"I believe he might have." Ben nodded as he spoke. "In fact, he *would* have. I'm sure of it."

Max swept the room with her eyes. "Let me ask all of you," she said. She looked across the room at Sam Little. Out of the corner of her eye she could see someone heading for the rear door. She waved at Henry but kept her eyes on Sam. "Why would someone open a door if he knew the man behind it had a shotgun and that man said he would shoot anyone who tried to come in?"

The person near the far wall stopped at the sight of Henry and turned around. Now he was on his way to the front door.

Max had to raise her voice to be heard over the sound of footsteps and falling furniture. "Unless," she said, "he knew that the man behind the door was dead. And no one would know Billy Ray was dead except whoever had shot him two hours before." Her last words were lost in a cry of pain and panic as Margie knocked Ivan to the floor.

With a nod from Max, Henry walked to Ivan, holding his handcuffs.

"How about that," Sam said.

"Ivan had looked at the garage when he put a price on the place," Brenda said. "So he knew the lock on that window was broken."

Margie was behind Ivan, twisting one arm up. Ivan was wincing in pain. Margie smiled at Max and said, "Guess I've still got it." She lowered his arm long enough for Henry to put the cuffs on Ivan, who leaned against the wall with his head down.

Max looked out to Main Street just as the OPP van arrived from Cranston. Well, that was fun, she told herself. Now the paperwork needs to be done.

———

"That was," Henry said as he picked at the last of Margie's lasagna, "the best bit of police work done outside of Toronto." It was almost midnight, and the Port Ainslie police station was well lit on a dark Muskoka night.

"Those OPP guys don't care what we did to nail Ivan as the killer," Max said. "They don't agree he should be charged right away. They want to question him on their own. They don't think we could have done what they're supposed to do." She grinned. "But we did."

"Did you hear that one guy," Henry said, "the big sergeant? Did you hear him say he would have worked it out himself, right away? About Ivan opening the garage door, I mean. He said it wouldn't have taken him all day to work it out. He would have known it was Ivan as soon as he heard Ivan opened the door."

"Maybe he might have got it," Max said. "But I didn't. Not until I went out to see Deborah Edwards at Rockcliffe Point."

"What did that prove?" Margie said. They had eaten lasagna, apple strudel, cheddar cheese and hot coffee, all brought from Margie's kitchen. They couldn't stop talking about the day's events.

"Didn't prove a thing," Max said. She got up to fill her coffee mug. "It just sent me back to Ivan's tale. About how he opened the garage door. It hadn't sounded right, but I didn't know why. Then, when I heard he had walked on the shore at Rockcliffe Point, I knew he had lied to me. He said he had been there looking for land to build the resort on. It would be plan B for the resort if Billy Ray wouldn't sell his land. But that didn't make sense. No one would build a family resort there. There's no beach and no room for buildings. Who would pay big bucks to stay in a place like that? So I had to ask myself why he was there."

"To toss away the gun," Henry said. "Throw it into the lake. They'll be dragging the water for it first thing in the morning."

"The gun he told you had been stolen," Margie added.

"That's when I thought about the garage door," Max said. "Driving back from the Point, it all became clear."

Margie said, "I'll bet that show-off OPP cop wouldn't have put things together the way you did."

"And I'll bet the town council will have more respect for you now that you solved a murder all on your own," Henry said.

Max thought about that. Then she said with a smile, "You know what? I don't think I care anymore."

And they still, she knew, would call her Max.

She didn't care about that anymore either.

JOHN LAWRENCE REYNOLDS has had thirty works of award-winning fiction and nonfiction published. *A Murder for Max* is his first book in the Maxine Benson Mystery series. He lives in Burlington, Ontario, with his wife, Judith.

AN EXCERPT FROM

MURDER BELOW ZERO

A MAXINE BENSON MYSTERY

BY JOHN LAWRENCE REYNOLDS

COMING FALL 2017

ONE

"You wouldn't be upset if this were January," Margie Burns said.

"I wouldn't be upset if this was Baffin Island either," Maxine Benson said. "But it's not. It's June in Muskoka and I have to wear a sweater, which is wrong. All wrong."

It was early on a Monday morning, just past seven.

Winter had been mild and almost free of snow. Everyone looked forward to a soft spring and a hot summer. "That's the way it works around here," they said. "Shiver in January, swelter in June."

But summer was staying away, and so were the tourists. On the second morning in June snow fell on top of Granite Mountain and lawns shone with frost. "It's just a cold snap," people said. "Be gone soon." But now it was the middle of June, and the cold remained. People began saying to each other, "Tell me again about global warming—I could use a laugh."

"These things happen," Margie said. "The weather has its own mind, you know. We just have to give it time."

"I'd like to give it hell," Henry Wojack said. He had finished his coffee and was blowing into his cupped hands.

"Well, you must admit," Margie said, "people behave themselves in this weather. Makes our job easier. If things get slower around here, we'll all have to retire." She was making her weekly report on crime in

Port Ainslie. There was never much to report, but so far there was even less than usual.

Bruce Orville Peter Chadwick, known as Bop, spent Tuesday night in a jail cell for being drunk in a public place. The truth was, he had been sober. It would be too cold for Bop to sleep in the park that night, so he had asked Margie to let him sleep in the corner cell, his favourite. Margie said she couldn't do it unless she booked him for a crime. Bop swore he was drunk, so Margie said, "Okay," and asked how he would like his eggs in the morning.

There had been a break-in at a cottage down the lake, but the owners said nothing was taken. A power generator was stolen from a home on Creek Road. Max had to tell a teenage rock band to close their garage door when they were playing. Even with the garage door closed, they were still loud, but no one seemed to care. A dog had run through the town without a leash.

Everyone knew the dog's owner was old Dale Carter, so Max called, told him where to find his dog. "Take it home and keep it tied up," she said. Carter felt so guilty that he sent Max a box of chocolates for her trouble. And a week ago a woman called to report her husband was missing. He had been gone two days. His name, she said, was Robert Morton. Max had passed this to the Ontario Provincial Police, who handled serious crimes. A missing person was serious, but Max knew that most missing people turned up within a few days. She and Henry and Margie dealt with small matters. Like dogs running loose, petty theft and loud rock bands.

"Less trouble than normal this week, thanks to the cold weather," Margie said. She closed the report book. "I swear they have more crime over at the St. Marks bridge club."

Max and Henry stood looking out the window. They had finished their coffee and morning chat. Now there was not much to do but watch people pass by on Main Street. Most wore winter jackets, scarves, hats and gloves.

Which is when the phone rang.

Max hit the phone's speaker button and said, "Port Ainslie Police Department, Chief Benson here." Max liked to say her title aloud. She was the only female police chief in Muskoka, and she wanted everyone to know it.

A woman's panicky voice sounded from the phone's speaker. "There's…" she began. She started over. "There is a man lying in the ditch on Bridge Road, near Elm Street."

Where, Max wondered, was Bop Chadwick? "Is he drunk"? she said.

"I don't know," the woman asked. Her voice was lower and more steady. "I mean, he is naked. And dead. And the body is frozen stiff."

"If this is someone's idea of a joke about the weather," Margie said while Max and Henry grabbed their jackets and ran for the door, "they have gone too far."

The door slammed and the sirens began as the cruisers pulled away, heading for Bridge Road.

"Much too far."